MW00977572

Hudson

Hudson

by Ruth Narrod

Gissia De Moya

Published by Themis Publishing
Chicago, Illinois

ISBN: 0-9660780-0-4
Library of Congress Catalog Card Number: 97-61996

Printed in the United States of America
December 1997

Written by Ruth Narrod
Illustrated by Diane Johnson

To Tia

Special Thanks to
the French Fry Woman

Green River Farm was home to a Grandma, a Grandpa, and two dogs. The dogs were about to become parents.

Neither animal had been a parent before, so they were a bit nervous. Especially Waverly, the soon-to-be dad.

The farm was big enough so that Waverly and Marla, who was expecting her new puppies to come any minute now, could run without seeing the end of the grounds. But it was small enough so they never got lost.

Marla was lying in the dogs' favorite resting spot inside the big, red barn. Waverly never liked to go in through the open doors. Instead he always jumped on top of two stacks of hay piled outside one of the windows, and leaped into the open window onto more soft, piled hay. Some barns don't even have windows; luckily, this one did.

Whenever Waverly got nervous, he ate. In fact, he had just finished eating a tuna fish and jelly sandwich that the woman who lived on the farm had made for him.

Usually the barn made him feel safe and relaxed. But because his nerves were getting the best of him, he walked out the open barn doors. He walked right past the hay stacks without even thinking about jumping back in.

Waverly roamed now because he knew that if he was nervous, he should try to do something else to take his mind off things.

"Hmmm," he thought, "my mouth is dry." Just at that moment he looked down toward his paws and spotted a Hudson Rootbeer can. "What a lucky day," he thought as he pulled his favorite soft drink toward him. He tipped the dented can and slurped up the last few drops.

Just as Waverly swallowed his last sip of rootbeer, he heard Marla yell out, "Waverly, darling, it's time!" It was about to happen. Waverly stood foolishly for a second, not knowing quite what to do. Then he shook himself, turned around, and ran as fast as he could back to the barn, the Hudson Rootbeer can still dangling in his mouth.

Marla had a litter of five puppies. As soon as they were born, the puppies stopped yelping and rested quietly against their mother, who also fell asleep after all her hard work.

"Aren't they cute!" Waverly turned his head toward the excited voice that burst into the barn. It was Kate, an 8-year-old with hair the color of strawberries. Actually, Kate's hair was almost exactly the same color as Waverly's. Three of the newborn puppies nestling happily in the hay were the shade of sand. The other two puppies were chocolate-colored.

"They're absolutely dear," answered Kate's grandma, who followed Kate into the barn. Kate's grandma made wonderful tuna fish and jelly sandwiches. "But we must be quiet so that we don't wake them," her grandma said. Kate tightened her lips. She pretended to lock her mouth closed, then threw away an imaginary key. Grandma squeezed Kate next to her and said, "Your mother said you could have one. We'll keep the rest."

"Can I pick one now?" Kate asked.

"You don't have to," Grandma said, "not until they get a little bit bigger. When your summer vacation's over and it's time to go home."

"I already know the one I want," Kate said. She pointed toward the runt of the litter, one of the golden ones, who looked like he had only half a left ear. He was awake now and playing with Waverly's can of Hudson Rootbeer, which was also Kate's favorite drink. Kate walked softly toward the puppies, and gently knelt down beside them. She touched the smallest puppy's nose ever so gently and said, "His name will be Hudson. And he can come live with us. Right, boy?"

Kate looked down at Hudson's big, brown eyes and laughed as his wet tongue slurped against her fingers.

"Looks like you found yourself a friend, Katherine," Grandpa said as he walked inside the barn. Grandpa was the only one Kate allowed to call her Katherine. (Kate was a very headstrong 8-year-old.) But she loved Grandpa so much it didn't bother her. Whenever Grandpa spoke, his words sounded so loving.

Kate ran toward Grandpa and into his open arms. She held him tight and said, "I could squeeze you 'til the poop comes out."

"Kate!" Grandma yelled. Kate let out a hearty giggle.

"Your mother is resting a bit," said Grandpa, "so I thought the two of us could take a walk." Kate's smile suddenly disappeared as she said, "Mom is always tired."

"I expect that your mother will be tired a bit longer, at least until the baby's born," Grandpa said. "So you might need to pull out the 'P' from your back pocket."

"What 'P', Grandpa?"

"The 'P' is for patience," Grandpa explained.

"Don't worry, I'll help Mom," Kate said.

Grandpa winked at Kate and said, "That a girl."

"My mom and dad told me a million, zillion times that I was going to have a new baby sister or brother," Kate said. "And they told me I would always be special. They told me since I'd be the big sister, I would need to teach the baby things."

"Sounds as if you've thought out the situation quite clearly, Katherine," Grandpa said. "But you forgot one very important thing."

Kate raised her eyebrow, just like she always did when she didn't fully understand something. "What'd I forget?"

"You will also always be my first grandchild, Kate."

And that was the only time Kate could remember her grandfather ever calling her Kate. "Now don't get me wrong, I'll love the new baby a lot, but," Grandpa tapped on his heart, "this ticker's big enough for both of you."

"Kate!" yelled her mother. Kate's mom was walking a bit slowly with her hand on her big belly. Kate ran toward her mother. "How's my special girl?" Kate's mom asked.

"Good," Kate answered politely.

"Oh, the puppies have arrived," Kate's mom said excitedly.

"C'mon," Kate said as she grabbed her mother's hand. "I'll show you the one who's going to be ours."

"Holy cat!" Kate's mom said. Kate's mom said that ever since the time Kate asked her why people always said "Holy cow." Her mom couldn't come up with an answer, so she started using any word but cow. Sometimes, Kate's mom said, "Holy tree!" or "Holy snake." Anything but cow.

Of course, Kate was bigger now, and she understood that sometimes expressions just came to be. Still, she liked when her mom took her questions seriously.

Kate led her mom to the puppies.

"They're adorable," her mom said.

"He's the one I want, Mom," Kate said, pointing to Hudson, who was sleeping again and breathing very quickly, like puppies do.

"Remember, sweetie, that this puppy is going to be a part of our family for a very long time, so make sure he's the one you want."

"No question about it," Kate said earnestly, "Hudson's the one for us."

Kate's mom smiled. "Oh, I almost forgot," she said as she dug into her big jacket pockets and pulled out a cold can of Hudson Rootbeer. "I thought you might want this."

"Thanks," Kate said as she popped the can open.

Kate's mom looked down at Hudson's big, brown eyes. "Hudson it'll be then. When, of course..."

"I know, I know," Kate interrupted her mother, "when he's bigger."

Kate's mom smiled.

* * * * *

Vacation was over and school was about to begin. Usually that brought a frown to Kate's face but not this time. Hudson was here now.

Kate never had a dog before, so she couldn't compare Hudson to any other dog, but she was sure he had to be the smartest dog in the whole world.

Of course, Hudson had learned all the usual dog commands. He could sit, heel, and stay. All on command. But more importantly, he could catch a Frisbee.

"Wow! What a catch!" Kate exclaimed when Hudson jumped into the air to catch a less-than-perfect throw by Kate.

Kate ran over to Hudson and squeezed him tight. "You're the best dog ever!" she said as Hudson wagged his tail. Then she took the red bandanna off her head and loosely wrapped it around Hudson's neck.

The bandanna was her good luck charm, and she wanted Hudson to have it from now on.

Hudson knew that Kate's bandanna was special to her, so he wagged his tail especially hard and brushed against her tan legs.

"Kate's a thoughtful girl," thought Hudson. She brushed him regularly so his hair didn't collect in nasty clumps, and she always found him when his favorite cartoons were on TV. Kate must love him very much.

Of course, at first Hudson missed Waverly and Marla. But, when he was getting ready to move into his new home, his parents had explained to him that in this world, adult people raise children, and children raise puppies. "Sometimes you've got to go down a road," his mother had told him. "There will be roadblocks. Or maybe the road will bend. But you've got to find your own way." Waverly added, "Hudson, you're going to move in with some lovely people."

His parents had rubbed up against Hudson and gently nudged him toward Kate. "We'll always love you," they said as he drove away with the Wilkes family.

* * * * *

"Hudson! Look out!" Kate yelled as she watched the neon-green Frisbee she had awkwardly thrown and which was about to land in some spindly branches. Hudson snapped out of his thoughts to jump up high and catch the floating Frisbee.

"That a boy!" praised Kate as Hudson made the catch. Then Kate looked sheepishly at Hudson. "Sorry, Hudson. I'm not so great at throwing Frisbees. But by next summer, I'm bound to get better."

Kate noticed that Hudson didn't look as pleased with her kind words as he usually did. And he didn't bring the Frisbee to her and drop it at her feet. "Something's wrong," Kate said out loud.

Walking briskly to see what wasn't right, Kate saw Hudson's head turned cockeyed, trying to pull something caught in his fur. He was wincing. It was then that Kate spotted a thorn stuck in Hudson's side. Very gently, Kate removed the thorn as Hudson gave a brief yelp.

"I'm sorry, Hudson," Kate said with sad eyes. Hudson looked up at Kate with a forgiving look as Kate hugged him. She picked up the Frisbee, which now lay near Hudson's paw, and carelessly threw it behind her. She then lay down beside Hudson and plucked a blade of grass. She kissed Hudson on the head, popped the grass in the corner of her mouth, and sighed.

"Kate! Hudson!" they heard Kate's mom yell. "Lunch time!"

Kate walked through the porch screen door. Hudson, however, preferred to go through the Plexiglas trap door made especially for him. He headed directly to his metal bowl full of fresh, cold water and slurped it up quickly. Catching Kate's sloppy throws made him very thirsty.

Hudson walked over to the corner of the porch and lay on the floor. Kate, on the other hand, sat down at the glass table in front of the two tuna fish and jelly sandwiches set there. She lifted one of the sandwiches off the plate and gave it to Hudson.

Kate's grandma and grandpa had told her mom what Hudson's favorite food probably would be. Of course, they were right.

"Holy baby!" yelled Kate's mom as she joined them on the porch.

"What is it, Mom?" Kate asked, startled.

"Our baby just gave me one hoot of a kick."

"You're okay, aren't you?" Kate asked, trying to convince herself.

"Of course, honey. Come feel." And Kate put her hand gently on her mother's big belly and felt something pound against her hand. Her eyes grew wide as saucers.

"You hear that, Hudson?" Kate asked. "We're going to have a new baby in the family soon." Hudson tapped his tail against the floor.

Suddenly there was a very loud noise. Hudson jumped up and started barking. Kate dropped her sandwich onto the floor, and her mom knocked over an empty glass. Then Hudson cocked his head, trying to determine what was happening.

"Ouch! M&M!!!" screamed Kate's father from down in the basement.

Kate's mom let out a hearty chuckle and looked at Hudson. "Don't worry, Hudson, it's only Kate's silly father. He must have dropped something on his foot—again."

"Or hit his thumb with the hammer again," said Kate as she dusted off her sandwich and plopped it back onto her plate.

"Or gotten," added Kate's mom with a gleam in her eye, "his tie caught in the vice again. His name sure isn't 'Grace,' is it, Kate?"

"Nestle's Crunch!" yelled Kate's dad. Kate looked at her mom and they both started laughing.

Kate's dad never swore. Instead, he yelled out the names of candy bars when he felt the need to let off steam.

"I just wanted to make sure you were all awake," joked Kate's dad as he lumbered onto the porch, his arms loaded with 2-by-4 pieces of wood.

Dad looked at Hudson, who still looked a bit puzzled by all the commotion.

"I'm going to build a dog house, right below your tree house, Kate." Dad was acting as if he never dropped anything, like he was a master carpenter—which he wasn't.

Kate ran up to him. "What a terrific idea, Dad!" She seemed to forget her father's fumble fingers.

"I'm going to get started on the dog house right away," announced Kate's dad. Kate walked over to Hudson. "Hear that, boy, you're going to have your own special house." Even a dog needs time to himself. Hudson wagged his tail.

"Holy horse," yelled Kate's mom.

"Did the baby kick you again, dear?" asked Kate's father.

"I think our baby is anxious to come into the world."

Kate's dad walked over to her and gave her a big hug. "But you'll always be my special girl," he said as he kissed her head.

"What do you say we all go out for ice cream?" suggested Kate's mom.

"Yippee!" yelled Kate.

"Dear, Kate hasn't even finished her sandwich," her father said.

Kate gulped down the last bite of her sandwich. "Omm fshid, Dud," Kate said. What she meant was, "I'm finished, Dad." Her father, of course, understood her perfectly.

He chuckled and said, "Ice cream it is then."

Kate and her mom and dad left the house without even noticing that Hudson had gone to his water bowl for a drink and found it empty. He looked around, a bit puzzled, and then went back to the corner of the porch and licked the spot where the thorn had been stuck earlier.

* * * * *

Kate was finishing up a banana split at the Ice Cream Palace.

"This is the best day of my life," Kate beamed.

"And I have a hunch it's about to get better," announced Kate's mom.

Kate raised her eyebrow and asked, "Is it finally time for my new brother or sister to come?"

Kate's mom said with a heavy sigh, "I think it's almost time."

* * * * *

A week later, the baby was finally born. When Jack came home from the hospital, he didn't have much hair, and the little hair he did have stood up in a funny sort of point. And just like his dad, Jack had two different-colored eyebrows—one brown and one blond. Kate was already looking forward to teasing Jack—when her father wasn't around, of course.

Kate's mom seemed even more tired after Jack was born. Because the kid never seemed to sleep. He just cried all night long. Kate thought he must be part owl by the late hours he kept.

At first, Hudson thought the baby was cute. But now, the poor dog was always too tired since he wasn't getting his proper rest with all the racket every night. Everyone was getting cranky, which wasn't like the Wilkes family at all.

One night, when Jack awoke crying again, Hudson went into the baby's room to try to quiet him before he woke everyone else. Hudson performed silly tricks in hopes of quieting Jack. He played dead, tried to shake Jack's tiny hand through the crib, and even attempted a somersault. Still, Jack continued to cry. And cry. He got louder and louder, until his face was bright red.

Kate's dad ran into Jack's room in his rumpled pajamas to see what the trouble was. Moments later, Kate appeared, dragging her feet and wiping her eyes with the backs of her hands. Then Kate's mom shuffled in her fuzzy yellow slippers. She had deep, dark circles under her eyes. Hudson thought she looked like a prize fighter with two black eyes.

Kate's dad cracked his knuckles loudly.

"Dear, will you please stop that," Kate's mom scolded him.

"Oops," she said as she bumped into Jack's crib, making him cry even louder.

"Gosh darn it, Hudson!" Mr. Wilkes scolded as he tripped over Hudson.

"Huh?" thought Hudson.

"Did you wake Jack up again?" he demanded.

"Awe, poor baby Jack," Kate's mom said as she gently picked up the baby.

"What's going on here?" thought Hudson. Had Mr. Wilkes really said, "Gosh darn it?" Not "Clark bar" or "Baby Ruth"? And Hudson was getting a little sick of hearing everyone always say, "Poor baby Jack." After all, what about him? Hudson started to leave the room when Kate's mom tiredly said from the rocking chair, "I'm very disappointed in you, Hudson."

"Gosh, Hudson, and Dad was going to build you a dog house and everything," Kate said. Hudson left Jack's room and went downstairs by himself. He was feeling too sorry for himself to even watch TV in the family room. He walked outside to roam around, and didn't come back for hours. He felt very lonely.

The next morning, when Hudson arrived home for breakfast, everyone seemed in better spirits. Baby Jack was happily gurgling in his little baby chair. Kate was munching on her favorite breakfast: waffles with strawberry syrup. And Mr. Wilkes was refilling Hudson's water bowl.

"Sorry I was gruff last night, Hudson," he said. "guess we've all been tired lately." He patted Hudson on the head as Hudson wagged his tail forgivingly.

Mr. Wilkes then opened up the door to the porch so Hudson could go out for a morning run. He started to go out his trap door, but Jack's mechanical swing was in the way. For a second, Hudson was starting to think Jack was in the way.

Kate used to walk Hudson every morning. But since Jack was born, Kate just let Hudson out. And it used to be that when Hudson brought in the morning paper, Mr. Wilkes would say "Thank you" and give him a dog biscuit. But lately he had forgotten his manners and didn't say anything. And Kate's mom used to play tug of war with him with a squeaky dog toy she had bought him.

She hadn't bought him anything in a while. Not that Hudson just wanted "things." He wanted a little more attention. "Yep, things are definitely changing around here," thought Hudson.

Kate's dad finally noticed that Hudson couldn't get out. "Sorry, boy," he said as he moved Jack's swing out of the way. Hudson didn't even look up. He just crawled through the door. Hudson was feeling rather sorry for himself.

Hudson wasn't supposed to leave the yard by himself. But at the moment he didn't care about any silly rules. The Wilkeses were afraid he'd get hit by a car. "Oh, yeah, like they really care," thought Hudson.

Hudson easily pushed open the gate latch with his nose. He didn't know why he hadn't done it before. Then he started on his way down the street. It looked as if everyone had just mowed their lawns. Everything seemed to be in its place.

Hudson started walking with his nose toward the ground, sniffing for the scent of other dogs. "Hey!" barked another dog. "Hey, yourself," Hudson responded.

The other dog, a little Yorkshire terrier, had knocked down a garbage can and was eating from its spilled contents. "Yuck!" Hudson blurted out.

The terrier ignored Hudson's outburst. "What's your name?" the dog asked between bites.

"Hudson. What's yours?"

"Queeg," the terrier snapped back. "Not that it's any concern of yours."

Hudson hadn't thought his day could get any worse, but now even a stranger was talking rudely to him.

"Where are you going?" Queeg asked gruffly.

Hudson hadn't thought about where he was going. He was just wandering. He couldn't think of a response.

"I know about the new baby," Queeg said. "It's all over the neighborhood."

"What about the new baby?" Hudson asked, puzzled.

"Oh, you know," Queeg said with a wink. "You're kind of in the way now. Not that the Wilkes want to tell you. They probably feel sorry for you. But the way I hear it, 'Baby in; Hudson out.'"

"What do you mean?" Hudson asked worriedly.

"Does the Wilkes family treat you well since the baby was born?" Queeg asked.

"They're okay," Hudson said slowly. "I mean, everything's not exactly the same, but there are bound to be some changes."

"Sure, sure. You say that now. But just wait. The changes will get worse."

"They will?" asked Hudson.

"Definitely," Queeg said confidently. "I bet they yell at you a lot more, then apologize."

Hudson thought back to last night, and then this morning. They had all blamed him for going into Jack's room when he was just trying to help. And then Mr. Wilkes had said he was sorry this morning. But, still, Jack's baby chair was in front of *his* dog door just moments later. Maybe Queeg was right.

"You know what I think you should do?" Queeg asked.

Hudson just shook his head sadly.

"I think you should come with me. Not that I normally take time to help other dogs, but in this case I feel sorry for you," Queeg cocked his head, and added, "since no one really likes you..."

"Kate likes me," Hudson said, not fully convinced.

"The girl? Hmmm," Queeg said. "Word has it that she used to take you for walks. Now she just lets you run out on your own where you could get hit by a car or something. I mean, if I wasn't looking out for you..."

It was too sad for Hudson to even think about Kate not liking him.

Queeg started to walk away, then turned his head back toward Hudson, who was just standing there in a daze. "No one else is going to care about you," Queeg said, "but like I said, because you're so pitiful, I'll help you."

"You're right," Hudson said sadly. "I won't stay where I'm only in the way."

* * * * *

"Hudson!" yelled Mr. Wilkes. "Come back, boy!" yelled Kate out the front door.

"Where do you think Hudson went, Dad?" Kate asked.

"Oh, I'm sure he'll be back soon."

"But, Dad," Kate said, "he got out of the yard and he might get run over or get lost or something."

"What do you say you and I go out and look for him," Mr. Wilkes suggested.

"Okay," Kate said, sniffing back a few scared tears.

Mr. Wilkes tried to be brave for Kate's sake, but he was worried. Hudson was still a puppy and he really didn't know how to take care of himself yet.

* * * * *

Hudson and Queeg had walked for hours. Hudson didn't know where he was any more. Nothing looked familiar. There weren't many houses. Instead there were tall apartment and office buildings, and alleys, and busy streets.

"Where are we?" Hudson asked.

"If I had any idea just how dumb you were, I never would have agreed to help you," Queeg said sourly.

Hudson sighed deeply. "Maybe Queeg doesn't know where we are either," he thought. "Maybe I shouldn't have left home," he said out loud to Queeg.

"You know, Hudson, I didn't think you could get any dumber, but I was wrong. That's the dumbest thing you or anyone else has ever said. I didn't want to tell you this, but I heard the Wilkeses were planning on getting rid of you soon anyway."

"How do you know?" Hudson asked rather defensively.

Queeg thought for a minute. "Did the baby cry a lot at night?"

"Yes," Hudson answered.

"That's because, and I didn't want to have to be the one to tell you," Queeg said, "but he's allergic to you. So the Wilkeses were going to have to give you away. It's not like they were going to keep you over the baby."

"Well, I guess that's it," Hudson agreed with Queeg. "I can never go home again. I'm on my own."

Just then Hudson heard a loud noise. It was his stomach growling.

"I'm hungry," Hudson said.

"Yeah, well," Queeg said, "you're on your own, Hudson. You're holding me back." And with that, Queeg ran off down the street. Hudson was all alone.

Hudson swallowed hard. He was scared. He couldn't go home even if he wanted to because he was lost. Besides, the Wilkeses were going to get rid of him anyway. So even if he could find his way back, it'd be no use.

It was getting late. "I'd better find a place to sleep before it's dark," Hudson thought.

Hudson had never been out on his own before. In the dark, everything seemed scarier. He felt so alone. He moved his head from side to side and felt the bandanna around his neck that Kate had given him. "And I thought she liked me," he thought.

Hudson found a torn cardboard box in an alley and crawled into it. He closed his eyes and tried to sleep. But there were so many sounds in the city. They whirled all around him.

There were sirens blaring, and horns honking, and people screaming. Each different sound made Hudson more frightened. He was used to the quiet of the Wilkeses' house—except for Jack, of course.

He must have fallen asleep, and as soon as the sun rose, Hudson crawled out of his cardboard box. Although he was scared to venture out to explore his new surroundings, he was very hungry.

He started walking down the long city block to find something to eat. "Right now, I could go for a bite of Kate's waffles," Hudson thought. Then he shook his head as if to rid himself of those thoughts. "That's the past; it's time to move on," he told himself.

Hudson had never felt his stomach so empty before. It was even too empty now to gurgle. His paws were raw from so much walking on the hard concrete. Just when he thought he couldn't take another step, he spotted a fruit stand. Grapes, bananas, apples, kiwi, and watermelon were piled high on wooden crates. "Finally, something to eat," thought Hudson.

He hopped on his hind legs and helped himself to a banana. He returned to all fours and started to peel it back with his teeth. Just as he was about to take his first bite, he saw the lady grocer come out from the store behind the stand. He put the banana down and was about to say "Thank you" when she started yelling, "Give that back! I won't have you dogs stealing from me!"

Hudson didn't exactly mean to steal the banana. But he could never remember being so hungry. He just wasn't thinking. Now he picked up the banana with his teeth and ran as fast as he could. The lady grocer was screaming, waving a broom in her hand.

"I better not see you around my stand again!" yelled the lady.

Just when Hudson thought he was done for, he turned into an alley. He stopped for a moment to listen for the lady's screams.

"Dog, you had better watch out," the woman said faintly. Soon Hudson couldn't hear the lady's words at all.

"Whew!" said Hudson. He was just about to take a bite of the banana, when he realized that he had lost it.

Hudson plopped down in the alley. "I'm so hungry," he said sadly.

"Here," said a voice. Hudson looked behind him and saw a black Labrador retriever standing a few feet away. The Lab pushed a piece of bread Hudson's way.

Hudson forgot his manners and wolfed down the bread without introducing himself. But he was so hungry he couldn't help it. In fact, he ate the bread so quickly that he didn't even notice that it was stale.

As Hudson was finishing off the bread, the Lab shoved a crumpled bag of chips toward Hudson. Hudson looked up for half a second, barked out a quick, "Thanks," then dug his nose into the bag of chips.

The Lab nodded and looked at the haggard-looking Hudson wolfing down his food.

As soon as Hudson had finished eating, he looked up at the Lab gratefully.

"What's your name, kid?" the Lab asked.

“Hudson.” Hudson was a little embarrassed now about not being more polite.

“I’m Glencoe,” the Lab said. “And you’re welcome.” Hudson smiled at the first friendly face he’d seen in this harsh place.

“You’re new to the streets, aren’t you, Hudson?” Glencoe asked.

“What do you mean?” Hudson asked, trying to sound tough.

Glencoe shrugged. “You tryin’ to make it hard on all us dogs? We can’t have the neighborhood grocers against us.”

“But, I was hungry,” Hudson explained. “I just took a banana.”

“Well, they don’t like you just helping yourself like that,” Glencoe said. “Makes people a little queasy, like you’re spittin’ on the fruit or somethin’. Come on,” he said, “I’ll take you where you can get something to eat. Besides a stale piece of bread.”

Hudson and Glencoe started walking down the street. Hudson noticed some small children holding their ears. “I guess the noise bothers them too,” Hudson said.

"You'll get used to it," Glencoe said. "After a while, you won't even notice the noise. Hey look!"

Hudson looked ahead of him and saw an organ grinder with a monkey on his shoulder. "Maybe the city isn't all bad," thought Hudson.

"Hey there, Glencoe," said the organ grinder. "How you doing boy? Haven't seen you in a while," he said as he patted Glencoe on the head. "I see you found a friend."

Hudson cringed a bit as the organ grinder lowered his hand.

"Don't worry, boy, no one's going to hurt you here," the organ grinder said as he gently patted Hudson. Hudson wagged his tail.

"Glencoe," said the organ grinder, "I have a little treat for you and your friend." He dug into his pocket, pulled out two dog snaps, and handed them to the monkey. "Give one to each of our friends," the organ grinder told his monkey. And with that the monkey gave Glencoe and Hudson a dog treat.

"Now this is more like it, isn't it, Hudson?" Glencoe asked.

Hudson nodded weakly.

"Guess you can't appreciate things until you've got some more food in you," Glencoe said.

"You've said a mouthful," Hudson said with a smile.

Glencoe and Hudson nodded good-bye to the organ grinder and his monkey, then walked on and turned the corner. All of a sudden there was a rich smell of freshly baked bread. Hudson inhaled deeply. "It smells delicious," he said.

"We'll go around back of the bakery," said Glencoe. "They always throw out stuff that they don't think looks perfect."

Hudson and Glencoe went around back. Sure enough, they saw a man in a chocolate-stained apron tossing bread and cookies and who knew what else into a big blue Dumpster.

"Everything sure looks perfect to me," Hudson said as drool formed in the corner of his mouth.

"It is," said Glencoe, "but people are just plain silly sometimes. They throw away things that are perfectly good."

Hudson and Glencoe waited a second or two to watch the baker return to the store. As soon as the metal door clanged behind him, they ran to the Dumpster.

"Shoot, usually there's a crate to hop on," Glencoe said.

"No problem," Hudson said as he took a running leap and hopped on top of the Dumpster. He picked up a few sugar cookies and tossed them down to Glencoe. Then he found some jelly donuts.

For a split second he thought of Kate's tuna fish and jelly sandwiches. Then he returned to digging in the Dumpster. What luck! There was a coffee cake. He picked it up with his teeth and threw it to Glencoe.

"Come on, eat," Glencoe said. Hudson jumped down. "You first," Hudson said politely. He had forgotten his manners once before and didn't intend to do it again.

Glencoe smiled and took a bite. Then Hudson began eating very, very quickly.

"Slow down," Glencoe said. "You're going to make yourself sick."

Hudson couldn't slow down. He was just plain too hungry. He ate two jelly donuts, four sugar cookies, and half of the coffee cake.

Hudson looked at Glencoe. His friend hadn't eaten much. "What's wrong?" he asked.

"Nothing," Glencoe said. He just stared at Hudson, which made Hudson rather nervous. Finally, Glencoe asked, "Why did you leave home?"

Hudson was surprised by such a direct question.

"I don't want to talk about it," he said.

"Okay then," Glencoe said. "Come on, Hudson, we should get going before the baker comes out again."

Just as Hudson and Glencoe turned the corner, they heard the baker come out and toss another tray full of goodies into the Dumpster.

Hudson was full, but Glencoe told him they should go back for a few more. "You can never tell when your next meal will come," Glencoe told him.

* * * * *

The Wilkeses sat at the picnic table in their back yard.

"I'm not hungry," Kate said as she played with her spaghetti.

"Not eating isn't going to help us find Hudson," her dad said gently.

"I bet Hudson is hungry," Kate said.

Mr. Wilkes put his fork down. Suddenly he didn't feel much like eating either.

* * * * *

Hudson let out a huge belch after gulping down two blueberry muffins. “Excuse me,” he said, embarrassed.

“My, don’t hurt yourself!” Glencoe teased. Hudson was getting sleepy. At home, he liked to take a nap after eating, but he didn’t know where he could get in a good nap here in his new surroundings.

Glencoe seemed to read Hudson’s mind. “Come on,” he said. “Let’s take a load off at my place.”

Glencoe and Hudson walked a few blocks. They heard a train coming. Hudson started to walk across the tracks since the train looked quite a distance away.

“Careful,” snapped Glencoe, tripping his friend to stop him.

The two dogs glared at each other.

“You’ve got to learn to be more careful,” Glencoe said, very seriously. “The train always looks farther away than it is.”

All of a sudden the train whizzed right past them. Hudson nearly lost his breath.

Once the train passed, they quickly crossed the tracks. To his left, Hudson saw a rather dirty-looking river.

“I live just over there,” Glencoe said.

They walked under a bridge next to the river. Hudson saw several trash cans knocked on their sides, empty food containers, old-looking pieces of clothing, and four dogs hanging out among the mess.

Glencoe introduced Hudson to the four dogs.

There was Jarrod, a big St. Bernard who had drool running from the corners of his mouth. He was chatting with Buffalo, a feisty-looking Cocker Spaniel. Buffalo spoke excitedly, wagging his tail in emphasis, while Jarrod listened quietly. Buffalo would occasionally shake his entire body as if to rid himself of Jarrod's floating, shedding hair. Mason, a Rottweiler, was walking round and round in circles, while Cody, a Basset hound with especially long ears, just seemed to watch—and listen.

The dogs all looked a little skinny and underfed, Hudson thought. And while the dogs looked to be friends among themselves, they all seemed to be on guard. None of them looked completely relaxed.

Watching the other dogs suddenly made Hudson feel very, very tired.

"What do you say we get a little shuteye?" Glencoe suggested.

"I'm not tired," Hudson lied. Then his eyes closed, even though he was still standing. "Well, maybe I am—just a little," he said.

Hudson and Glencoe lay down on a flat piece of dirty cardboard.

"Can I ask you a question?" Hudson asked Glencoe as they lay there, heavier. Dusk was falling all around them.

"You just did," teased Glencoe.

"Another one?"

"There you go again," said Glencoe. "Go on—ask a real question."

"How did you end up here? I mean, did you ever have a real home?" Hudson asked.

Glencoe sighed deeply.

"You don't have to tell me if you don't want to," Hudson said.

Glencoe smiled at Hudson. "It's okay." And then Glencoe started to explain. "I used to live with an old man."

"Was he mean to you?" interrupted Hudson.

"Oh, no. He was very kind to me. He was a groundskeeper at a private school. He took care of the lawns, the flowers—stuff like that. I lived with him in a little apartment above a garage."

"So why did you leave?" Hudson asked.

"Like I was saying. He was very kind to me. He worked the grounds and let me run around. Sometimes he took me over to where the school kids were playing. They found sticks and threw them to me. I loved running and bringing them back to them just so we could play again. Each time I brought the stick back Mr. George would stop raking or doing whatever he was doing and say to the children, 'Isn't my friend Glencoe a great dog?' and all the children would nod their heads.

"One time," Glencoe said, "and I don't mean to brag, but a boy about nine years old fell into the pond. Some very young children saw him fall and were standing by the water pointing. But they were too scared to do anything. I saw a rope that Mr. George had used earlier to tie up a tree to a pole so it wouldn't get knocked down in the wind. I grabbed the rope and threw it to the boy who was drowning. I held onto the rope with my teeth as hard as I could. The little kids were screaming for the boy to try to grab the rope. And just as the boy was about to go completely under the water, he grabbed the rope. Some kids were crying. And then I heard Mr. George."

"What did he say?" Hudson asked. His tired eyes were suddenly wide open again.

"He didn't know what was going on at this point. He was kind of talking to himself, saying, 'Now where did I put that rope?' And then he saw the kids standing by the water. He ran over and saw the boy hanging onto the rope. He took the rope out of my mouth and towed the boy in."

"Was the boy okay?" Hudson asked.

"Yeah, but he was pretty scared," Glencoe said.

"But he's okay, right?" Hudson asked again, worriedly.

"He's okay," Glencoe assured him. "Anyway, my gums were bleeding from the rope and all the children left to talk with the boy, who was still shaking from having nearly drowned. But Mr. George stayed with me and kept telling me over and over again how I had saved the boy's life."

"And you did!" Hudson exclaimed.

"I know," Glencoe quietly said.

"I still don't understand why you left, then."

"Well, it was in the newspapers and everything how I had saved the boy's life. And everything was going great. But the excitement or something must have gotten to Mr. George because he died shortly after that."

"So they made you leave even after you saved a student's life?" Hudson asked angrily.

"Not exactly," Glencoe explained. "The school got a new groundskeeper. He was much younger than Mr. George. And he tried to be nice to me but he wasn't like Mr. George and he never will be," Glencoe said. Then after a moment he said, "So I left."

Hudson was getting very tired. “Goodnight, Glencoe.”

“Goodnight,” Glencoe answered.

* * * * *

Hudson awoke to something dripping on his face. He opened his eyes slowly expecting to find rain. But he quickly discovered it wasn't rain.

"Yuck!" Hudson exclaimed. Jarrod, the St. Bernard, was standing over him drooling. Glencoe started laughing as Hudson shook his face dry.

But the laugh was on Glencoe because he was suddenly surrounded by an awful smell. Mason, the Rottweiler, was breathing heavily on him.

"Oooh, Mason, you've really got to do something about that halitosis of yours," said Glencoe.

Mason looked at Glencoe confused. "What are holly toes?" Mason asked Glencoe.

"Halitosis," Glencoe explained, "is your breath—bad."

Mason's feelings looked hurt. So Glencoe gently said, "It's not your fault, Mason. You just need a dog biscuit."

Since Cody was listening, he popped in with an idea. "What do you say we go to the baseball stadium?"

Hudson sat up. He had never been to a real baseball stadium, though he had watched baseball on TV. Buffalo wagged his tail excitedly. "Yeah, we'll eat hot dogs and popcorn and if we're lucky, some nachos."

Hudson's stomach growled just thinking about it. He could already picture them all sitting behind the bleachers gorging themselves. The only thing he didn't know was that he'd be eating people's leftovers.

* * * * *

Kate nailed up her last flyer to a telephone pole just a few yards from her house. It had a picture of Hudson and said, "My dog is lost—please help me find him," and it gave her telephone number. She'd made the flyers herself.

"Kate!" yelled her dad from their backyard. "What do you think of your tree house?"

Kate ran back toward her dad. "You're right, Dad," she said. "It's perfect."

"All right then," said Mr. Wilkes. He then took out a hammer and pounded one last nail into the tree house. "Baby Ruth!" screamed Mr. Wilkes as he accidentally hit his thumb instead of the nail.

"You okay, Dad?" Kate asked.

"Yes, sweetie," said Mr. Wilkes.

"Dad," Kate asked, "do you think someone will call us about Hudson?"

"If we're lucky, sweetie," Mr. Wilkes said.

* * * * *

Hudson, Glencoe, Jarrod, Mason, Cody, and Buffalo were off to see a baseball game. Glencoe had explained to Hudson that some people thought baseball was a game that was too slow. But Glencoe thought that maybe some people were just plain moving too fast.

When they got just outside the stadium, Hudson and his new friends spotted a lot of vendors.

"Popcorn! Peanuts! C'mon and get your peanuts!" yelled one vendor who had a ferret sitting next to him. Other vendors were selling hot dogs, balloons, rubber balls, t-shirts, and even dog sweaters.

"I definitely need a dog sweater," Cody said. All the other dogs just looked at Cody oddly.

"Well, I do," Cody said flatly.

Hudson thought dog sweaters were silly. Dogs had enough fur to keep them warm, and the sweaters only seemed to amuse dog owners. "Not that I even have a dog owner anymore," Hudson thought.

Suddenly a man was screaming and pointing at Hudson and the rest of the dogs.

"Get out of here, you pack of dogs, before you're sorry!" the man screamed.

Hudson was very frightened of the man's mean-looking eyes. But Glencoe wasn't afraid. He stood there bravely.

"Sometimes, people just act mean because no one's ever taught them to be nice," Glencoe whispered to Hudson. "Watch, if I go over there and nuzzle against his leg, he'll see we don't mean any harm." So Glencoe started over, but then out of nowhere, he felt a sharp pain in his side.

"Got him!" A young boy sneered at the dogs and then ran away holding a slingshot. Glencoe fell to the ground in pain.

"Nice shot, kid!" the man yelled after the boy.

All five dogs helped get the bleeding Glencoe to a far corner of the stadium.

As Hudson and Mason tried to lick Glencoe's deep wound, Hudson said, "Let's face it, people are just plain mean."

"Now, Hudson," Glencoe reprimanded, "your friend Kate wasn't mean. Only a puppy would say something so silly."

"Well, I am a puppy," Hudson said indignantly.

"Of course you are, but in order for you to grow up to be a good, strong dog, you need to work on being more mature," Glencoe said as he winced from the sting where the rock had hit him.

Mason suddenly got up and started going round in circles again. Whenever Mason got nervous he just kept walking round and round. That was because he had lived with a family that hadn't treated him very well. One time, when Mason's owner had taken him to dog obedience school, all the dogs were supposed to walk in a circle. One dog in front of the other. But Mason kept getting mixed up. After class, Mason's owner made him walk in a chalk circle over and over again. Each time he stepped outside of the circle, Mason's owner kicked him in the side. One time after he was kicked especially hard, Mason ran away.

His owners never even bothered to look for him. Glencoe fell asleep under the bleachers. Hudson thought that maybe the pain had knocked him out. Hudson shook his own body as if to rid it of unpleasant thoughts. And it worked. He looked up to see Jarrod looking at him, smiling and drooling. He was kicking a used paper cup. And, of course, right behind Jarrod was Jarrod's shadow, Buffalo, who was shaking off Jarrod's ever-shedding hair.

Hudson felt something at his feet. He looked down and spotted Cody's long ears against his legs.

"What do you think we should do about Glencoe?" Cody asked.

At first Hudson thought, "How should I know? I'm only a puppy." But then he remembered Glencoe's words. He had to start thinking for himself. And he had to look out for Glencoe while he was hurt.

So Hudson told Cody to go ask Jarrod for his paper cup.

"When you get the cup, go stand by the drinking fountain over there," Hudson told Cody, pointing with his paw. "Be sure to look as pitiful as possible with the empty paper cup in your mouth."

"Should I try to fill it up?" Cody asked.

"You won't be able to reach the water," Hudson explained. "But if you hold it in your mouth, maybe a boy or girl will offer to fill it for you."

Hudson was right. Not even a minute passed before a small boy noticed Cody. "Thirsty, boy?" asked the child.

Cody wagged his tail and tried to look as pitiful as possible. And it worked. The boy gently took the slobbery cup from Cody's mouth and filled it with water. He then set it down for Cody to drink.

But Cody didn't drink any of it.

"What's the matter, aren't you thirsty?" the boy asked. Of course Cody couldn't explain that he had gotten the water for Glencoe, so the young boy simply shrugged and went on his way.

Once the boy had left, Cody very carefully picked up the cup full of water, hardly spilling a drop, brought it back to the bleachers, and set it down near Glencoe, who had just woken up. He was still in too much pain to slurp much of the water, but Hudson encouraged him.

"C'mon, Glencoe, drink up. You never know where your next drink is going to come from." Glencoe smiled weakly at Hudson and then took a few sips.

"Good job," said Hudson. "Now just rest a bit more and you'll be better in no time at all."

* * * * *

"Dad, a lady is on the phone. She found Hudson! She's bringing him over."

At the sound of Kate's happy news, Mr. and Mrs. Wilkes jumped off their chairs. Even baby Jack gurgled happily as he heard the news while fingering a squeaky dog toy that Mrs. Wilkes had bought right after Hudson disappeared.

"Jack, honey, that toy belongs to Hudson. Here's your rattle," said Mrs. Wilkes, handing the baby his own toy.

A little while later, the doorbell rang. Kate ran to the door, with the rest of the family right behind her.

When Kate opened the front door she saw a woman with a huge beehive hairdo, holding a small Pekinese dog.

"That's not Hudson!" Kate said rudely as she ran away from the woman. Mr. and Mrs. Wilkes just stood there, embarrassed and disappointed.

* * * * *

Hudson removed the bandanna from around his neck. With his teeth, he tied it around Glencoe's neck.

"It's for good luck," Hudson explained.

Glencoe smiled. "Hold on," said Hudson. "I'll be right back." Hudson kept his word, and was back in a few moments with a large, flat piece of cardboard in his teeth. Hudson then nudged Glencoe onto the cardboard.

"We're not going to be at a baseball game without you seeing it right," Hudson said as he carefully dragged Glencoe several yards to behind home plate. It was the best seat in the house!

"Now as soon as I get us something to eat, the day will be perfect," Hudson beamed. "Besides, I've never heard of anyone not feeling totally better after eating a hot dog." Hudson climbed out from under the bleachers and walked to a teenage vendor.

"Hot dogs!" the girl cried. "Get your hot dogs here!" Then she looked down at Hudson.

"Hungry, boy?" she asked kindly. Hudson wagged his tail enthusiastically.

"You know, you look just like my dog, Wiley." Then the vendor squatted down and offered Hudson a steaming hot dog. But Hudson closed his mouth tightly and kept his tail still.

"It's okay," the girl said. "I saw your friend under the bleacher. Don't worry, my dad owns this stand. He loves dogs and he won't mind me sharing a little food with you and your friend. Honest."

Hudson looked up. "My name's Bo," the girl said as she rubbed Hudson's side. "It's not my real name. My real name's Grace Jean—I hate it. So I named myself after Bo Jackson." She moved the hot dog again toward Hudson's mouth. Bo nodded her head and said, "C'mon, just a bite." Then Bo set the hot dog down in front of Hudson. As Hudson gobbled it up, Bo went back behind the stand, packed up a few hot dogs, and opened a bag of chips. She put the food in a small cardboard box.

"Hey, Dad!" Bo yelled to her father, who seemed to be somewhere behind her. "Can you watch the stand for just a minute?"

The girl's father looked at his daughter, then down at Hudson, who still had a trace of mustard on his lips. He smiled. "Okay, just for a minute," he said as he patted Hudson on the head.

Hudson looked up at Bo. "C'mon boy," she said as she reached down to grab his collar. But Hudson didn't have a collar.

"You should have a collar with your name on it, boy," Bo said. "I'm sure some family misses you and I can't call them if I don't know your name."

Hudson, of course, couldn't tell Bo his name. Besides, Hudson thought as he looked sadly down at his feet, he remembered Queeg's talk of how the Wilkes family no longer wanted him.

"Let's go to your friend," Bo said.

As Hudson and Bo neared the bleachers, Glencoe looked up nervously.

Hudson quickly explained to Glencoe that Bo was just coming to deliver some food. Bo waited for Hudson to stop barking. Then she set the food in front of Glencoe, who slowly took a bite of a hot dog. Mason, Cody, Jarrod, and Buffalo all dug in with hearty appetites.

"You're hurt, aren't you, boy?" Bo asked. She then pulled out her wallet from her back pocket, took out a tissue, cleaned some blood off of Glencoe's fur, then took out a bandage and put it over Glencoe's slingshot wound. "My dad always makes me keep a bandage in my wallet, just in case," Bo explained. Then she gently patted Glencoe's head. "Don't worry, you'll be okay, as soon as you eat a little more. I wonder how this happened." Glencoe's mouth was full of hot dog.

Just at that moment, the boy who had hit Glencoe earlier with the slingshot walked past and Glencoe yelped. Bo ran out from under the bleachers and grabbed the boy by the shoulder.

"Hey! What are you doing with that thing?" she demanded, grabbing the boy's slingshot.

"Nothing," the boy lied. "Hey, give that back!"

Bo was at least a head taller than the boy, who looked a little scared. "Slingshots are *not* for hurting dogs," she told him. "Now get out of here!"

"But, the game's not over," whimpered the boy. Bo didn't soften. "Come back next week when you're feeling a little less...foolish."

The boy sulked as he walked toward the exit gate. Bo just shook her head and walked back to her hot dog stand.

* * * * *

Gene Hernandez was up at bat. He was the best hitter on the team, with two outs in the eighth inning, and he didn't let his fans down, hitting a home run. As soon as the ball flew over the stadium wall, colorful fireworks blared overhead. Hudson and Glencoe watched excitedly, then laid back contentedly for the rest of the game.

By the game's end, with the home team winning by five runs, all six dogs were full and very happy.

At the exact same moment, both Hudson and Jarrod let out a deep belch and everyone giggled. Then Mason, Jarrod, Cody, and Buffalo went off to stretch their legs. "We'll be right back," Mason called out as he began to chase his tail.

"Do you ever think about going home?" Hudson asked Glencoe when they were alone.

"I told you," Glencoe said, "Mr. George died. I have no home."

"I know that Mr. George died. But I was thinking that the new groundskeeper might be nice." Glencoe started to look in the distance.

"The new person may never replace Mr. George," Hudson continued, "but maybe you both could still learn to be friends."

"Do *you* ever think about going back home?" Glencoe asked defensively.

"I don't want to talk about it," said Hudson. But Glencoe looked hurt, so Hudson added, "I can't go home. They didn't want me there any more."

Glencoe didn't press Hudson for more information. He just said, "They must have been pretty awful."

Before Hudson could answer him, the other dogs came back. "Come on," yipped Buffalo happily, "let's go home."

They started toward the gate, feeling as full and happy as six pigs in cool mud.

All of a sudden, Hudson heard a familiar voice behind them. "Gee, a whole pack of losers."

Hudson turned around and saw Queeg leering at them.

* * * * *

"What do you want this time?" Glencoe demanded.

"You know him?" asked a surprised Hudson.

"Queeg and I go way back, don't we?" Glencoe said.

Queeg just stood there, looking a little dumb.

"Queeg was the one who told me how the new groundskeeper would never be as nice as Mr. George and that he didn't want me. Then he stole all the food I'd gathered and got me kicked out of a garage, right, Queeg?"

Queeg ignored Glencoe. "I heard the Wilkeses are getting on great since you checked out," he said to Hudson.

Quietly, but sounding quite angry, Glencoe said, "You have no idea how the Wilkeses are doing, do you, Queeg? In fact, you've made up everything you ever said to any of us, haven't you?"

With that, all six dogs bristled and bared their teeth, and Glencoe barked so loudly that Queeg cowered and ran off, muttering all the way.

"Let's get out of here," Glencoe said.

But Hudson felt funny, as if someone was watching them. He looked around, but saw nothing. Suddenly they turned a corner.

It was Queeg again. But this time he was with his friends. And he had a lot of them. They all seemed very mean and very angry. Some of the dogs with Queeg looked as if they had been starved. Some had open wounds, and all bared their teeth.

Hudson looked around for an escape. But there was none. Queeg and his friends had them trapped. Hudson thought back to his parents' words. "There will be roadblocks. But you've got to find your own way." Hudson quickly racked his brain. He didn't want to fight, but he knew there was no other way. Still, he thought he should try to talk to Queeg first—dog to dog.

"Queeg, there's no point in fighting. We'll all end up getting hurt and feeling bad, so what do you say you and your friends go your way, and my friends and I will go our way. And we'll forget this whole thing ever happened."

"You forgot one small detail, Hilson," Queeg said.

"Hudson," Hudson corrected.

Queeg continued. "The point is, I don't like you and my friends and I won't be the ones getting hurt, it'll be you ending up licking your wounds."

Hudson never liked the idea of fighting. It seemed so silly. "Heck, I'd walk away from this whole mess if I could, but I can't," Hudson thought sadly. But then he became determined and thought, "If I can't walk away, I'll just have to walk through it." Hudson looked around him. More of Queeg's friends had gathered. But he was no longer scared. Instead he looked to Mason, Jarrod, Cody, and Buffalo.

And then Hudson looked to Glencoe. "We can do it," Glencoe said. "But we've got to look out for Buffalo and Cody, who are smaller than us."

Hudson looked at his friend admiringly. Even after being hurt earlier, he still cared more about his friends than himself.

"I can't let anything more happen to Mason," Hudson said. "He's been through enough."

"I'll be okay," Mason said as he breathed his bad breath on Hudson and Glencoe.

"No, Mason, Hudson's right," Glencoe said. "Besides, we need you to watch after Buffalo and

Cody. Now go on," Glencoe said. Then Glencoe looked to Hudson.

"Ready?" Glencoe asked.

"Ready," Hudson said.

* * * * *

"Kate, you can't give up, just because something doesn't come easily to you," Mr. Wilkes advised.

"I don't want to Dad, but I don't know what more to do. I mean, we've put up flyers. I've asked everyone in the neighborhood if they've seen Hudson. I know it's all my fault," Kate sniffed.

"What do you mean?" Mr. Wilkes asked.

"I didn't walk Hudson as much as I should have. And I threw my Frisbee into some thorny branches, so it's no wonder Hudson didn't like me any more."

Mr. Wilkes sighed deeply. He and Kate were tired and sitting on a park bench after looking for Hudson all day. They were far from home, but they knew their search had to extend beyond their neighborhood. So the whole family went out to look for Hudson again. They looked every morning before school, after school, and again after dinner. But still no luck. They simply couldn't find Hudson.

"It's not your fault, Kate," Mr. Wilkes said. "Actually, I'm afraid it's my fault."

"What do you mean?" Kate asked.

"Remember before Jack was born and we all wanted to be sure you knew how very much we loved you?"

"Yeah, so you told me a zillion trillion times that you wouldn't love the new baby more than me and that I'd never be in the way. All that stuff."

Mr. Wilkes smiled. "Exactly. And I'm afraid we didn't take the time to tell Hudson how *he'd* never be in the way."

Kate looked up at her dad, who looked very sad, and hugged him. "It's no one's fault," Kate said simply. "We'll just have to keep looking."

* * * * *

Hudson started walking confidently directly toward Queeg. Queeg snarled his teeth. Then the other dogs started barking.

"Just stay behind me," Hudson told Buffalo and Cody. "I'll try to divert their attention. And when I do, you get away from here as fast as you can."

"I'll take care of them," Mason said.

"We can't leave you," Cody and Buffalo said at the same time to Hudson.

"He'll be fine," Mason said. Though he had to admit he was a little afraid for both Hudson and Glencoe.

Hudson raised his head and continued walking directly toward Queeg. But Hudson didn't see a mean-looking German shepherd behind Queeg, getting ready to attack him.

The German shepherd's eyes were red and angry. He lunged forward ready to jump on top of Hudson, but midair he fell to the ground writhing in pain. Queeg darted forward but he too fell to the ground in pain. Then another and another of Queeg's dog friends fell to the ground, until the rest ran away.

Glencoe turned his head and spotted Joey, the boy who had hit him earlier with a slingshot. Glencoe started to cower, but then he heard the boy say, "Don't worry, boy, I promised Bo that I wouldn't hurt dogs any more, but I heard the mean dogs and I figured I owed you one."

Bo ran up toward Joey. "I know you told me to leave," Joey said, "but I heard those mean dogs," Joey said as his eyes filled with tears.

Bo put her hand on Joey's shoulder. "I know," she said trying to comfort him. Then Glencoe walked up to Joey and rubbed against his leg.

"I'm sorry," Joey said. Hudson, Mason, Buffalo, and Cody all came over wagging their tails.

"You're a good man, Joey," Bo said. "Have a rootbeer—it's on the house."

* * * * *

"So you're really going to go back there?" Hudson asked Glencoe. The two dogs sat watching Mason walk in circles and garbage float by in the river.

"Yeah, I figure I should give the new guy a try. I'm tired of living on the streets. And who knows, I might like the guy."

"I hope you do," Hudson said.

"Are you going to go back home?"

"I can't," Hudson said.

"But Queeg made up what he said," Glencoe said.

"Maybe," Hudson answered, "but it's still true."

"Then why don't you come with me. We've got plenty of room," Glencoe said.

"Thanks, but I'll be fine." Hudson did not sound very convincing.

Glencoe turned his head and untied the bandanna that Hudson had given him earlier. "I think you need this more than me," Glencoe said. "Take care of yourself, okay?"

"Don't worry about me," Hudson said, taking the bandanna back with his teeth. "I'll be okay."

* * * * *

Hudson was walking in the park with his friends Mason, Jarrod, Buffalo, and Cody.

Hudson spotted a neon-green Frisbee caught in a small tree. He jumped up to reach it—careful not to get hurt by the branches.

Hudson threw the Frisbee with his teeth to Jarrod, who slobbered all over it. Hudson slowly turned his head. He heard a familiar voice.

"I love Hudson so much and now he'll never know it," a girl said.

Hudson knew that voice.

Kate spotted Hudson looking at her and ran toward him and hugged him.

"Holy fire hydrant!" Mrs. Wilkes exclaimed as she shifted Jack to her other hip. Mr. Wilkes threw his arms up with joy.

"I'm sorry, Hudson," Mr. Wilkes said. "We forgot to tell you how much you mean to our family." Mr. Wilkes paused. "You do, you know," Mr. Wilkes said.

Kate squeezed Hudson tighter. "I love you Hudson. I'm sorry I didn't take you for walks. I promise I'll never let you down again." Hudson wagged his tail delightedly.

"Holy tomato!" Mrs. Wilkes shrieked. "Jack and I almost forgot to give you something," Mrs. Wilkes said.

"Oh Jack, the one who replaced me," Hudson remembered.

Mrs. Wilkes put a new dog toy in Jack's tiny hand to give to Hudson. Jack handed it to Hudson who gently grabbed it with his teeth as Jack gurgled.

"It's for you. Jack has his toys; and you are to have yours." Mrs. Wilkes paused for a moment and then added, "I guess I had to get adjusted to little Jack and I got rather cranky and I unfairly took it out on you. I'm sorry, Hudson. You are as much a part of this family as Jack. And sometimes families make mistakes, but please try to forgive us and don't leave us again."

Jack gurgled at Hudson and Mrs. Wilkes bent Jack down to pet Hudson.

Hudson knew that he would never leave again.

* * * * *

At first Hudson had to get used to the new collar around his neck. The dog tags jingled as he walked. But the Wilkeses explained that just in case he ever got lost again, this time someone would be able to call them and they would come find him right away.

"Banana cake!" Mr. Wilkes yelled as the rest of the family heard the phone fall to the ground.

"Some things never change, do they, Hudson?" Mrs. Wilkes said, smiling.

"Who were you talking to, Dad?" Kate asked.

"I was just speaking to your grandparents, Kate. And they agreed to it," Mr. Wilkes said.

"Yippee!" Kate exclaimed as she ran up to her dad to give him a hug.

Mrs. Wilkes also smiled, but Hudson looked puzzled.

"Grandma and Grandpa want your friends to come live with them on their farm."

* * * * *

Hudson was just about to get in the Wilkeses' car when he saw Glencoe standing there.

"What are you doing here?" Hudson asked, surprised. "Was the new guy awful? Was he mean to you? Tell me," Hudson quickly said.

"Slow down. The new groundskeeper's name is Frank and he's very nice. He told me he wouldn't try to replace Mr. George. Instead he said he just wanted to be my friend. And he is, but I just wanted to make sure you were doing okay." Glencoe paused for a second. "I heard through the dog vine that you were back at the Wilkeses' and I wanted to make sure that they were treating you okay."

"Hudson, I brought you a rootbeer and a dog biscuit before we go," Kate said.

"Well, I can see everything's okay, but remember, if you ever need me, just let me know," Glencoe said.

"And you make sure you do the same," Hudson said, a little teary-eyed.

* * * * *

The Wilkeses—including Hudson—drove together with Mason, Jarrod, Buffalo, and Cody up to Green River Farm.

"Of course, we have a big place and we'll be happy to take the dogs," Grandpa said.

Mr. Wilkes had warned Grandma that one of the dogs (Mason, of course) had a bit of a bad breath problem. Grandma had chuckled over the phone saying that Mason would then fast become Grandpa's special friend since Grandpa had lost his sense of smell some time ago. Mr. Wilkes also told Grandma that one of the dogs had an odd habit of running around and around in circles.

In fact, the first thing Mason did when he got out of the Wilkeses' car was start running around in a circle. When Grandpa saw this, he pointed to the track and said, "If you want to run in circles, that's okay with me." Mason wagged his tail and headed straight for the track. Grandpa laughed.

Jarrod ran over and began rubbing himself all over Grandpa's legs. "As for you, my shedding friend," Grandma said to Jarrod as she saw hairs flying everywhere, "Maybe if we give you a proper haircut, you won't shed quite so much."

Cody and Buffalo walked back to Hudson.

"Don't worry," Hudson said. "They'll take care of you until I'm back."

"Back?" Cody and Buffalo asked.

Hudson smiled. "Sure, I'll be back every summer with Kate."

With that, everyone smiled.

THE END

You can order more copies of *Hudson* direct from the publisher with the order form below.

Copies are $4.99 U.S. plus $1.50 shipping each. Illinois residents please add sales tax.

Please send payment in the form of a check or money order to:

Themis Publishing
2506 N. Clark St., Suite 108
Chicago, IL 60614

Please send me _____ copies of *Hudson*.

Name:____

Address:______________________________________

City:_______________State:________Zip:_________

Amount Enclosed:_________